P9-CQE-282

For Geoffrey Bock

Henry Holt and Company, *Publishers since 1866*
Henry Holt® is a registered trademark of Macmillan Publishing Group, LLC
175 Fifth Avenue, New York, NY 10010 • mackids.com

Copyright © 2018 by Edward Hemingway
All rights reserved.

Library of Congress Cataloging-in-Publication Data
Names: Hemingway, Edward, author, illustrator.
Title: Tough cookie : a Christmas story / Edward Hemingway.
Description: First edition. • New York : Christy Ottaviano Books, Henry Holt
and Company, 2018. • Summary: In this twist on The Gingerbread Boy, Cookie
teams up with Fox to try to become sweeter and faster, before learning that there is
a reason he is different. Includes recipes for Christmas cookies and Christmas ornaments.
Identifiers: LCCN 2018004252 • ISBN 9781627794411 (hardcover)
Subjects: • CYAC: Cookies—Fiction. • Foxes—Fiction. • Identity—Fiction. • Christmas—Fiction.
Classification: LCC PZ7.H377436 Tou 2018 • DDC [E]—dc23
LC record available at https://lccn.loc.gov/2018004252

Our books may be purchased in bulk for promotional, educational, or business use.
Please contact your local bookseller or the Macmillan Corporate and Premium Sales Department at
(800) 221-7945 ext. 5442 or by e-mail at MacmillanSpecialMarkets@macmillan.com.

First edition, 2018 / Designed by Patrick Collins
The art for this book was created with oils on board sprinkled with Adobe Photoshop.
Printed in China by Hung Hing Off-set Printing Co. Ltd., Heshan City, Guangdong Province

1 3 5 7 9 10 8 6 4 2

TOUGH COOKIE

A CHRISTMAS STORY

EDWARD HEMINGWAY

Christy Ottaviano Books

Henry Holt and Company • New York

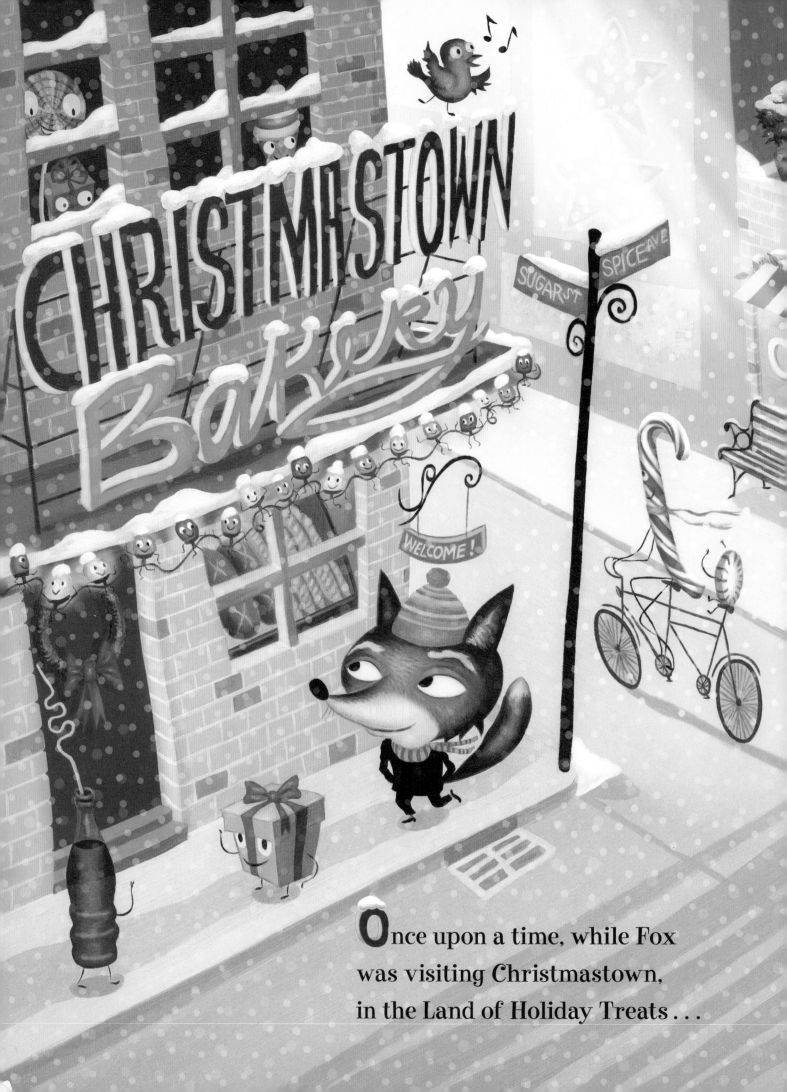

Once upon a time, while Fox
was visiting Christmastown,
in the Land of Holiday Treats . . .

Fox never could resist a challenge,
so he gave chase, shouting back,

You look very sweet.
Sweet enough to eat!

Fox was pretty fast.

And he loved sweets.

CRUNCH!

But Cookie wasn't sweet AT ALL—
and Fox spit him right out.

BLECH! YOU TASTE AWFUL!

How dare you!
I'm a SUGAR COOKIE. I taste WONDERFUL!

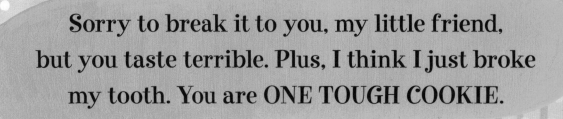

Sorry to break it to you, my little friend, but you taste terrible. Plus, I think I just broke my tooth. You are ONE TOUGH COOKIE.

But I'm sweet!

Um, no, you're not.

But if I'm not a sweet cookie, then what am I? A slowpoke who tastes terrible! What do I do now?

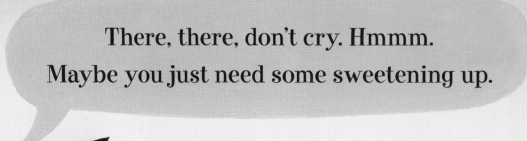

There, there, don't cry. Hmmm.
Maybe you just need some sweetening up.

You think so?

ORNAMENTS UNITE!

Decorati
hang toget

It's worth a try!

CHRISTMASTOWN
SPA

Elves!

DENTIST

SWEET
MASSAGE

OPEN

So after a quick trip to the
dentist to get his tooth fixed,
Fox took Cookie to the
Christmastown Spa,

where the elves dipped him
in delicious eggnog,

sprinkled him with powdered sugar,

and sang him sugary sweet
Christmas carols.

Fox gave him a lick, but Cookie still tasted terrible.

Hmm. You said you were a slowpoke.
Maybe we should work on your running instead?

So Fox signed up Cookie for the
Sweet Treat Christmas Race
that very afternoon, and
they headed for the park.

But Cookie's stubby legs and lack of experience made it impossible for him to keep up with the more seasoned runners.

And as hard as he tried . . .

Run, run, as fast as you can, Cookie!

FINISH

. . . he came
in last place.

Cookie was exhausted,
and he didn't feel so tough.
Was he cut out for anything?

Fox thought so.

Every treat in Christmastown
should be able to build itself
a proper gingerbread house.
You can, too. I'll help!

Okay!

So they found a nice little spot in the
gated community of Cookie Cutter and
got to work building
and decorating.

But when they were finished and Cookie
went inside his beautiful new home,

CRASH!

it didn't exactly hold up.

And that's when Cookie crumbled.

I'm not sweet.
I'm not fast.
I can't even make a
gingerbread house.
Everything I do
is half-baked!

Cookie finally knew what he was made of,

and he couldn't have been happier.

That afternoon he hung with care from a branch on the biggest Christmas tree in the center of the park,

with the sweetest
view in town.

Overjoyed, Cookie shouted
for all the world to hear:

Look, look, look at me!
You can't reach me—
I'm an ornament on a tree!

Make some room up there for me, Cookie!

Fox never could resist a challenge.

The end!

Cook up your own TOUGH COOKIES!

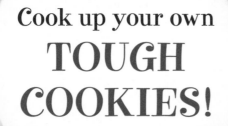

Template

TOUGH COOKIE RECIPE

(Delicious and gluten free!) Makes approximately a dozen cookies.

Ingredients

3 cups gluten-free flour blend

1 teaspoon baking soda

1 teaspoon ground cinnamon

1 teaspoon ground ginger

1/2 teaspoon ground nutmeg

1/2 teaspoon ground allspice

1/2 teaspoon ground cloves (Tough Cookie
would be naked without his cloves!)

1/2 teaspoon salt

1 stick (1/4 lb.) unsalted butter, softened

1/4 cup vegetable oil

1/2 cup light brown sugar

2/3 cup unsulfured molasses

1 teaspoon vanilla extract

1 large egg

Directions

1. Sift flour, baking soda, cinnamon, ginger, nutmeg, allspice, cloves, and salt together. Set aside.
2. Cream the butter and vegetable oil in a mixing bowl until well combined, about 2 minutes, then add brown sugar and mix for 1 minute. Add molasses, egg, and vanilla. Gradually add sifted flour mixture to wet ingredients and stir for approximately 1 minute, until it forms into dough.
3. Divide the dough into 2 equal parts. Roll each part into a ball and then flatten each ball into a disc. Store the discs in resealable bags and chill for at least 3 hours (or up to 2 days).
4. Preheat oven to 350° F.
5. Place each disc of dough on a clean, floured surface and roll out to 1/4" thickness. Using the Tough Cookie template above as a guide, cut into cookie forms. Transfer cookies to a nonstick or parchment-lined cookie sheet. Use all the dough by re-forming the excess and rolling it out again.
6. Place cookie sheet in preheated oven and bake for 7–10 minutes, until the cookie edges are light brown and firm. Remove from the oven and set on cooling racks for at least 5 minutes.

Icing and Decoration

Ingredients

2 egg whites

1 teaspoon vanilla extract

3-1/2 cups confectioners' sugar

Directions

1. In a mixing bowl, combine egg whites and vanilla and beat until frothy.
2. Add confectioners' sugar and blend gradually on low speed until the mixture is shiny.
3. Turn mixer to high speed and beat until stiff, glossy peaks form, approximately 5–7 minutes.
4. Transfer icing to a covered container and refrigerate for 1 hour. (Can be stored for up to 3 days.)

Decorating

Place enough icing into a small piping bag (with plain #2 tip) to create Tough Cookie's cuffs, hems, belt, and whites of the eyes. Add food coloring to icing to create red mouth lines and black eyebrows. For irises of the eyes, you can use dried currants, raisins, or coffee beans. The top half of small colored (red) mini gumdrops make great buttons. And if you're decorating cookie ornaments, a little red ribbon threaded through the hole in his head will help Tough Cookie hang with his pals on the Christmas tree!

TOUGH COOKIE ORNAMENT RECIPE

(non-edible) Makes approximately a dozen cookies.

Ingredients

2-1/2 cups all-purpose flour

1/2 cup fine kosher salt

2 tablespoons granulated sugar

1/4 cup ground cinnamon

1/8 cup ground cloves

1 teaspoon Tylose glue [optional]

1 cup warm water

Directions

1. Combine all ingredients except water in a stand mixing bowl. Mix with a paddle attachment on medium speed. (If you don't have a stand mixer, place ingredients in a regular bowl and mix by hand with a hard wooden spoon and a lot of elbow grease!)
2. Slowly add warm water until mixture works into a dough ball, approximately 2 minutes (longer if by hand).
3. Remove from mixer and transfer to a stainless bowl. Refrigerate for 30 minutes.
4. On a clean, floured surface, roll out dough to 1/4" thickness.
5. Use Tough Cookie template to create the desired cookie ornament shape. Place ornaments on a silicone pad or parchment-lined sheet pan. Don't forget to poke a hole in each forehead with the tip of a chopstick!
6. Bake at 250° F for 45 minutes. Remove from the oven to cool and dry for 1 hour.

Recipes created by Chef Michael Caracciolo, who has been creating and cooking culinary treats in the field of innovative cuisine for many years. You can find him online at privatechefbozeman.com. Photographs by Audrey Hall.